# MARTHA'S HOUSE

### By Edith Kunhardt
### Illustrated by Carolyn Bracken

### Golden Press • New York
Western Publishing Company, Inc., Racine, Wisconsin

Text copyright © 1982 by Western Publishing Company, Inc. Illustrations copyright © 1982 by Carolyn Bracken. All rights reserved. Printed in the U.S.A. No part of this book may be reproduced or copied in any form without written permission from the publisher. GOLDEN®, A FIRST LITTLE GOLDEN BOOK, and GOLDEN PRESS® are trademarks of Western Publishing Company, Inc. Library of Congress Catalog Card Number: 81-83005 ISBN 0-307-10120-7 / ISBN 0-307-68120-3 (lib. bdg.) A B C D E F G H I J

This is Martha.

This is Martha's house.

Martha hangs her hat
and coat in the front hall.

This is the living room,
where Martha and her father
play the piano.

In the kitchen Martha
helps with the cooking.

The workshop is in the basement.

Martha and her mother
are building a birdhouse.

This is the laundry room.
The washing machine and dryer are here.

Martha puts the soap
in the washing machine.

Here is Martha's bedroom.

Her special blanket and
animals are on the bed.

This is the bathroom.

Martha likes to
draw on the mirror
when it gets steamy.

The attic is at the top of the house.

Martha plays dress-up here on rainy days.

The garage is next to
Martha's house. Martha keeps
her tricycle here. Her mother
and father keep their car here.

In the back yard
there are swings, a slide,
and a sandbox.

"Good-by," says Martha.

"Come to my house again soon!"